Mess Monsters in the Garden

Beth Shoshan

Illustrated by
Piers Harper

meadowside
CHILDREN'S BOOKS

One day Mummy said
"*The garden's a mess!*"
And because it's so dirty
She suffers from stress.

I said,

"we need the dirt,
It's better – I know,
If it's tidy and clean
Then nothing will grow!"

But Mummy said "Nonsense!

That cannot be right!

I want nice paths and decking

And things to delight!"

What she didn't know

Was that locked in the shed

Was a big gang of monsters

From under my bed...

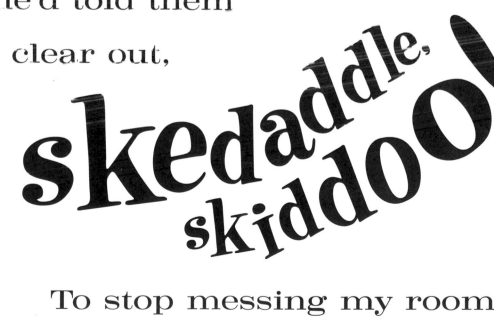

She'd told them

to clear out,

skedaddle, skiddoo!

To stop messing my room up

As they used to do.

First a **hook,**

then a Crook,

What a **hideous** sight,

As my **MOB** of Mess Monsters  into the light!

Those **monsterous monsters burst** up through the ground,

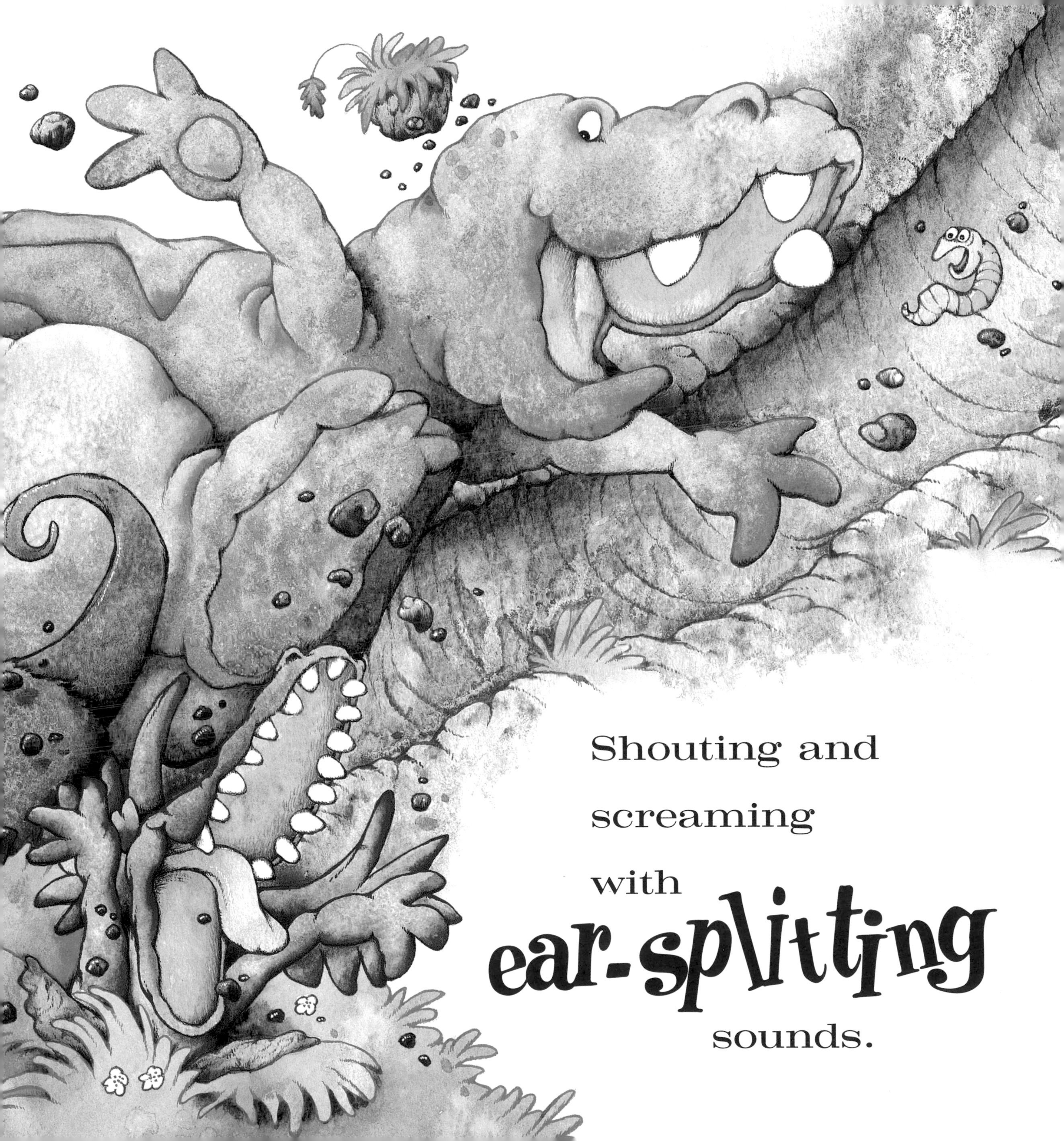

Shouting and
screaming
with
ear-splitting
sounds.

They **churned** and **upturned** the soil and the earth,

Throwing mud all about
them for all it was worth.

Even Teddy was ready

To lend them a paw.

But they **trashed** him

and **stomped** him,

And left him quite sore.

They dug up some toys
I was sure I had lost.
Then **crushed** them,

and **mashed** them,
Which made me quite cross.

I'd seen quite enough,

So I shouted,

Oi!

Stop!

And I handed a spade

To the monster on top...

So with bucket and fork
And a long garden hose,
Trying to avoid
any thorns in their toes,

They started to dig up

All over the place,

Throwing plants everywhere,

Getting mud in their face.

They scrabbled and scrambled
And worked through the night.

And when morning was here...

...what a fabulous sight!

Because...

Mummy was wrong

(Though we daren't tell her so!).

It's the mess in the garden

That makes gardens grow!

For
My Mummy
B.S.

For
Kate, Tim, Dan, Nick and Sadie
P.H.

First published in 2005
by Meadowside Children's Books
185 Fleet Street, London, EC4A 2HS.

Text Beth Shoshan, 2005
Illustrations © Piers Harper, 2005

A CIP catalogue record for this book
is available from the British Library.
Printed in U.A.E.

10 9 8 7 6 5 4 3 2 1